# Walt Disney's THE RESCUERS

## A GOLDEN BOOK • NEW YORK
Western Publishing Company, Inc., Racine, Wisconsin 53404

© 1977 Walt Disney Productions. All rights reserved. Printed in the U.S.A. Featuring characters from the Disney film suggested by the books by Margery Sharp, *The Rescuers* and *Miss Bianca*, published by Little, Brown & Company, Inc. No part of this book may be reproduced or copied in any form without written permission from the copyright owner. GOLDEN, GOLDEN & DESIGN, A GOLDEN BOOK, and A LITTLE GOLDEN BOOK are registered trademarks of Western Publishing Company, Inc.
ISBN: 0-307-00070-2    B C D E F G H I J K L M

"Bernard!" cried Bianca. "Your tail! It's all frizzy!"

Indeed, Bernard's tail *was* frizzy, for he was frightened. Bianca had chosen him to help her rescue Penny, a little girl who was in terrible trouble. They had just arrived at Devil's Bayou, where Penny was the prisoner of a horrible woman, Madame Medusa.

"Good luck!" said Ellie Mae and Luke, the friendly swamp folks who lived there.

"Thanks. We'll need it," declared Bernard.

Bernard's heart beat fast as Evinrude the dragonfly pushed the leaf-boat across the dark waters of the bayou and over to Madame Medusa's old riverboat.

He saw Madame Medusa shouting and raging and
waving a cane. Bernard shivered.

He also saw Snoops, who was Madame Medusa's
helper. Snoops was nearly as nasty as Medusa herself,
and he was sneaky and sly besides. Bernard quivered.

Then Bernard saw Madame Medusa's pets, and he shivered and quivered as though he would never stop. Medusa's pets were two crocodiles named Brutus and Nero. They had big scaly tails, sharp claws, and huge, long teeth.

"Bernard," whispered Bianca bravely, "we must save poor little Penny from these horrible creatures!"

Bernard gulped and nodded, and he and Bianca crept through the riverboat looking for Penny.

They found her shut up in a small room. She was sitting on a bed, hugging her teddy bear and trying to think of some way to escape.

When Bianca and Bernard saw Penny looking so sad, they became very angry. True, they were only small mice, but they did not approve of people who made little girls unhappy. They told Penny that they had come to rescue her.

Bernard called softly down to Evinrude. "Go and get Luke and Ellie Mae," he whispered. "Tell them we need help!"

Evinrude buzzed a brisk, brave buzz and sped off toward Luke's cozy old shack.

Evinrude was scarcely out of sight when Madame Medusa came storming in.

Quickly, Bernard and Bianca hid in Penny's pocket. And that was when they learned for the first time why Medusa was keeping Penny prisoner. Medusa was planning to lower Penny through a small opening into a cave where once, a long time ago, a pirate had hidden his treasure.

"Bring me the diamond called the Devil's Eye," Madame Medusa told the little girl, "and don't try any tricks. I'm going to keep your teddy bear until you get that jewel for me!"

Bernard was careful not to shiver or quiver when
Snoops and Medusa and the crocodiles marched Penny
off to the cave. He and Bianca hid in Penny's
dress pocket as she was lowered into the dark, dank,
dripping cave.

Penny looked around her, hoping to see where the
pirate had hidden the treasure. "Madame Medusa
won't let us out until we find the diamond," she said,
"and she might even hurt my teddy."

"Don't worry. We'll find the diamond," declared Bianca and Bernard. They squared their small shoulders and looked as courageous as small mice *can* look.

The search began. Bernard scooted and scurried and peeked and pried, and—at last—he found the diamond! He proudly gave it to Penny.

Quickly Penny called up to Medusa and Snoops. "I have it! I have it!" she cried.

Bernard and Bianca jumped back into Penny's pocket. Then Penny jumped into the bucket, and up, up, up they went to the opening of the cave.

Madame Medusa was delighted when she saw the diamond. So was Snoops. However, they were both so greedy that they quarreled and bickered over the diamond all the way back to the riverboat.

As the two big, ugly crocodiles herded Penny away, Bianca and Bernard hid in the tall swamp grass. Bernard almost wept. He and Bianca had tried so hard to rescue Penny, but they had failed.

"What can we *do?*" said Bernard. "We're only little mice."

"We can do plenty," said Bianca. "Just you wait!"

Suddenly there was a rustling in the grass. Luke and Ellie Mae had come. So had Owl and Rabbit. Turtle was hurrying slowly, as turtles do, and Mole was blinking his way along.

"We came to help," said dear, good Ellie Mae. "Maybe we *are* small, but if we small ones work together, who knows what will happen?"

So they all marched toward the riverboat, where a number of things happened very quickly:

First, Bianca and Bernard tricked the two horrid crocodiles into the elevator on the boat, and Rabbit helped to slam the door on them.

Then Owl, Mole, and Turtle lit a heap of fireworks on the boat. There was such a flashing and booming and crashing that silly old Snoops tumbled into the water, Madame Medusa screamed and scooted up a smokestack, and the boat started to sink.

Penny leaped into Madame Medusa's swampmobile.
So did Bernard and Bianca and Ellie Mae and Luke
and Rabbit and Owl and Mole. (Turtle was the last
aboard, as turtles often are.) They all sped away across
the bayou.

Penny was *so* happy! She was finally safe, and she
had her teddy bear again. She had the diamond, too,
because Madame Medusa had been foolish enough to
try to hide the jewel in the teddy bear.

"Bernard, you are *so* brave!" said Bianca.

"Oh, I'm not brave at all," said Bernard. "I was so frightened that my tail frizzed."

"You were brave even if your tail *did* frizz," Bianca said. "You did what was right, and that's what bravery really is!" Then Bianca smiled her nicest smile.

And do you know how happy this made Bernard? Perhaps you do—even though you've never been a small, frightened mouse!